Is My Family Crazy or Is It Me ?

Joseph McLean Hesh

NAVPRESS

A MINISTRY OF THE NAVIGATORS

P.O. BOX 6000, COLORADO SPRINGS, COLORADO 80934

The CROSSROADS Series Leader's Guide, a helpful one-volume guide for group leaders, is available from NavPress, and covers all four junior high discussion guides:

What's the Big Idea?
Swimming for Shore in a Sea of Sharks
Is My Family Crazy, or Is It Me?
Under the Influence

The Navigators is an international Christian organization. Jesus Christ gave His followers the Great Commission to go and make disciples (Matthew 28:19). The aim of The Navigators is to help fulfill that commission by multiplying laborers for Christ in every nation.

NavPress is the publishing ministry of The Navigators. NavPress publications are tools to help Christians grow. Although publications alone cannot make disciples or change lives, they can help believers learn biblical discipleship, and apply what they learn to their lives and ministries.

All Scripture quotations in this publication are from the *Holy Bible: New International Version* (NIV). Copyright © 1973, 1978, 1984, International Bible Society. Used by permission of Zondervan Bible Publishers.

Printed in the United States of America

CONTENTS

INTRODUCTION
Is My Family Crazy, or Is It Me?

The way they have this whole thing set up, you have to spend the first eighteen years of your life with a certain group of people who drive you crazy, known as your "family." Then, finally, you get to go out into the world and work hard to put together your *own* family to drive crazy!

For a lot of teens, family is a sore subject. But let's kind of step back and try to take a fair look at not only your parents and your brothers and sisters, but also at *you*, and how you relate to them.

Let's get right down to some nitty-gritty questions. What do you think of the whole *authority* scene? What about your *responsibilities* as a member of your family? What about problems in *communication*? And in your relationships with *brothers and sisters*? What about your *identity* within the family? And how about *slowing down the pace* a bit in your life?

These are the kinds of questions you can basically try to ignore because they make you uncomfortable, or you can try to get into them in order to get your life in focus . . . before you put together your *own* crazy family.

PLAYING TENNIS WITHOUT A NET
The Importance of Rules

◆ICEBREAKER
(Getting your brain in gear)

Play a simple group game, with the girls against the guys—but the girls get to change two major rules during the course of the game.

◆TUNE IN
(Checking out the situation)

My main games as a teenager involved bats, gloves, five-irons, and round balls. I didn't seriously pick up a tennis racket until I was 24 years old. At first, I went out on the court with a friend of mine just one time to goof off and hit the ball back and forth . . . and suddenly it clicked. "I think I could *like* this stuff!" Then I got out on the courts with a guy who was a former tennis pro. He taught me how to hit overheads, top spin, sliced backhand, baseline, cross-court. . . .

All of a sudden, tennis was fun. Hey, really, tennis is a great sport if you're thinking of giving it a try. They make balls of all different colors, and they make rackets with heads so big you could knock over cows if you wanted to.

Let's pretend that you and I are going out for a tennis match. Now, this isn't a nice, Sunday afternoon, "picnic in the park" game of just hitting the ball back and forth. No, this is blood and guts, championship of the world. We warm up, take a few practice serves, and then we're ready to play. After you blow me away in the first several games, it becomes apparent that you're going to hurt me badly in this game of tennis. So, while I'm losing 5-0 in the first set, I suggest that we try a new way to play the game. We will play without paying attention to the boundary lines. You get angry at this suggestion, but since you know I'm weird anyway, you think, "Why not? He's old and slow, and I can still take him."

You win the first set easily, and are on your way to a second-set victory, when I come up with another wonderful new rule: "Let's take down the net." Now you're really getting steamed. I mean, how can anyone play tennis like that? How do you score it? Where do you hit it? Where do you not hit it? When is the game over? Oh, we would still score it the same way . . . but without a net, tennis becomes an entirely different game than what you and I are used to.

After a while, it becomes evident that this new rule about no net favors me, the one with less skill . . . and the game simply isn't fun for you. You learned to play tennis the right way and you got pretty good at it. This second-rate version or imitation of the real thing just doesn't fit into your groove.

So, you lose interest and quit. And I win the "match"! You will call "foul" in my face for the days and weeks to come because you thought we were going to play tennis that day. And instead, we played some game that I made up so that I could win.

◆ JUMP IN
(Putting yourself in someone else's shoes)

1. Describe another game (for example, football) and what it would be like without rules. Would the game be enjoyable without rules?

2. Some games use an instant-replay camera to help with difficult decisions. Do you believe that this helps or hinders the enjoyment of those games? Explain why.

3. The reason why my opponent is angry in the tennis story is that:

    a. he wishes he had thought of these rule changes first. ❏
    b. tennis really isn't his favorite game. ❏
    c. he thinks I'm cheating and just making up new rules to help my own cause. ❏

    d. he has learned to enjoy tennis played the right way, and doesn't think the rules should be changed. ❏

4. Do you think a game's rules should ever be changed? Why or why not?

◆TIME OUT
(Looking at it from another point of view)

I enjoy playing "the ultimate survival game" with youth groups. Here's the situation: Your group has just survived an incredible disaster and you are the only remaining survivors on planet earth. All the natural environment — trees, crops, etc. — are okay . . . no contamination or anything . . . but you are the only survivors. There are no books, no televisions, nothing manmade. What do you do?

Groups go wild with this exercise. Some launch immediately into trying to form a whole new civilization. Some try to figure out who should marry whom, while others come up with some system for living together. But one thing comes out quite clearly: *Rules are needed to survive the game of life.* Just as tennis is not really tennis without a net, life is not life without certain rules.

What sparks the tension point in the teen mind today is the thought of, the restriction of, *and* the enforcement of rules. A person stays out after curfew and pays the consequences. Different families enforce different rules in different ways, so there's tension. "Johnny's mom let's him dress that way!" Instant conflict. Instant fight. What do we do?

One verse in the Bible that tends to depress teens in a major way is the one that says, "Children, obey your parents in the Lord, for this is right" (Ephesians 6:1). If only a different word than "obey" had been used, then I think teens would be happier campers—a word like "follow" or "learn from." But the word "obey" strikes powerfully at the heart of the teen. Yet, there is good reason for you to take a careful look at this verse.

First, rules are needed to survive the game of life. Agreed? Second, our homes have a strong influence on us, even in our teen years. In fact, they influence our thinking for many years to come. So, third, it really makes sense that the rules of the home have a powerful impact on us.

I haven't run into too many parents who really want to see their kids fail, fall apart, and be unable to cope with adult life. They just want to see you get the discipline needed to survive the low points: when you're out of money, out of a job, or perhaps in the middle of a relationship problem.

Discipline helps us contribute the best and enjoy the best in life. It goes beyond just toeing the line to get Dad off your back. It goes beyond just doing the right stuff to stay out of trouble. It influences the rest of your life to come. So, although it may not seem like it would be fun to obey and respond to authority—even in a positive way—remember that life has rules, just like tennis. And you can't just change the rules in the middle of the game! Successful living, and *happy* living, depends on your ability to play within the boundaries that make life what it is.

11

◆GET INTO IT
(Making the situation your own)

1. Describe the life of an eighteen-year-old who has *no* rules to live by in his house.

2. Describe someone else's home that you know of, in terms of the rules this person has to live by. Is it a better or worse situation than the one you're in?

3. How do you currently view your parents on the subject of authority and discipline?

   a. They're harsh. They just want to make life hard for me. ❏
   b. They're too busy with their jobs. I don't know what the rules are. ❏
   c. They're inconsistent. It drives me nuts! ❏
   d. They're strict, but I've learned to live with it. ❏
   e. They let me get away with murder. I'm having a great time! ❏

4. Does the word *obey* in Ephesians 6:1 — "Children, obey your parents in the Lord" — mean to you that you obey your parents in *everything*? What if they asked you to do something wrong?

◆ A WORD FROM GOD
(Getting the right message)

I run in the path of your commands, for you have set my heart free. (Psalm 119:32)

◆ FOR THE ROAD
(Taking something along with you)

Describe the rules you will give to your teenager when you're a parent. How are they different from the rules that you have to keep now?

HEY, WHERE'S THE STEERING WHEEL TO THIS CAR?
The Importance of Making Good Choices

◆ICEBREAKER
(Getting your brain in gear)

Time for a role exchange. All of a sudden *you* are the parents, and your parents are your teenagers! What are the things you now look forward to as a parent? What would you rather not deal with?

◆TUNE IN
(Checking out the situation)

Ah, that great rite of passage that you all look forward to: *learning to drive!* Some junior highers have already had the opportunity to pull a car from the driveway into (and through!) the garage. Some could probably do pretty fair if they were driving a car in a race—like maybe the Kentucky Derby! But, hey, you can't beat the fact that cars are cool, and looking forward to driving them is also cool. . . . So, since you and I want to be cool, we think about cars and driving during the junior high years!

Let's pretend that I'm your dad, and that I make zillions of dollars a year. I'm a famous television celebrity (of course) and we have a house that's as big as your high school, complete with swimming pool, Jacuzzi, tennis courts, golf course, gold mines, missile launchers . . . . Hey, you name it, we got it. You've just turned sixteen, got your driver's license on the third try, and we have a family celebration. In honor of your achievement, I, your father, give you the keys to a brand new, cherry red Lamborghini. Your jaw hits the cement. You're simply ecstatic! You jump up and down so hard that your dandruff comes loose.

You call all your friends and tell them you're going to pick them up. Then, as you turn the ignition key, tears come to your eyes as you hear the masterful sound of an engine that will simply blow the doors off anything in the state. You start daydreaming about doing 150 mph through normal residential neighborhoods. As you put this monster machine in reverse and turn your head to look down the driveway, you notice suddenly that . . . there's no steering wheel!

Hey, just a minor detail, right? No big deal! You've got an engine that could pull a freight train, a cherry-red finish that gleams in the afternoon sun, and . . . no steering wheel. Now, I am your father, but you have learned that when you show ingratitude, I usually ground you for a decade and tell you all these stories about how life was when I was your age. "Why, I used to walk to school fifty miles at a crack, uphill both ways." You just yawn and nod.

But this is serious stuff! No steering wheel! So, you figure the best thing to do is to play dumb. After putting the car in park and leaving the engine running, you come inside and give me a big hug and tell me that this is the best present you'll ever get in your whole life. You explain that the technology on the dash is so advanced that it boggles your mind. In fact, you tell me that I must have a superior technological mind to be able to bring it home and into the driveway.

After buttering me up that way for a while, you calmly state that you can't find the steering wheel. I start laughing. I say, "There *is* no steering wheel!"

Of course, you wonder if this is some kind of gag, so you ask how the car is to be steered. I say that there is no steering mechanism and that it can't be steered. Okay. How does one drive a car like that? Suddenly, this confused, empty feeling kicks up in your gut. What do you do?

◆ JUMP IN
(Putting yourself in someone else's shoes)

1. Our student hero in the story — *you* — should probably:

a. tie up your dad in chains and lock him in a closet. ❏
b. drive the Lamborghini anyway. Steering is no big deal! ❏
c. immediately try to sell the car for quick bucks. ❏
d. have your friends come over and put a steering column in the car. ❏
e. move to the mountains of Tibet and meditate on the hidden meaning of this story. ❏
f. borrow the family Rolls Royce and go pick up your friends. ❏

2. The father in the story—*me*—is:

a. mean. I'm playing a bad joke on my child. ❏
b. crafty. There is a point to this, and this is a trick question. ❏
c. dumb. Cars need steering wheels, and I bought a car without one. ❏
d. insane. I should seek professional help. ❏

3. Why is it important to have a steering wheel in a car?

◆TIME OUT
(Looking at it from another point of view)

Stan was like a bull in a china shop. He was the football team's main running back, but he was also an excellent blocker. We developed a strange kind of relationship in school . . . never really clicking as friends, but hanging out with the same people. Stan always talked with a lot of energy about what he wanted to do, where he wanted to go, and who he wanted to do it with. His claim to fame was having as his girlfriend the prettiest and most popular girl in school.

You've heard this kind of story before. Stan started to make acquaintances who were a lot older, and who were into some strange stuff. One of their hobbies was armed robbery. Not the kind of weekend fun most of us are into. And, the night that Stan was shot and killed in an armed robbery attempt, a lot of us asked some big questions about him and about ourselves. I wondered why it was that some teens have all the energy in the world, but they head off in a direction that simply doesn't make sense. Stan wasn't a Christian, but his sudden and surprising death made both believers and unbelievers wonder.

Sarah, on the other hand, was a believer. She, too, had incredible energy, but found herself in a different kind of dilemma. She had the right friends and was going the right way, and yet, one day woke up to realize she was maxed out—involved in band, choir, youth group, basketball team, and holding down a part-time job. Sarah was able to survive during her teen years but now asks if all her commitments were smart ones.

In both these stories, we see examples of cars without steering wheels. A lot of teens today want to be involved in a whole mess of things and yet have no clear-cut direction or system of priorities. And so, they merge into their adult world still playing all their options, but making no firm commitments. My generation has produced a crop of irresponsible adults who serve as role models to the teens of today! No wonder young people are confused. Yet, the hard reality is simply that *to live is to choose.*

You're in your early teens, at a crossroads of life. Without some kind of steering device, you won't really be able to choose what road you take. God has just the steering mechanism you need. But you need to *ask* Him to give you that steering wheel. Sometimes you get anxious to arrive at that glorious age of independence, even if your life has no steering wheel at all. Just don't wait until you're cruising at 150 mph and you can't steer the energy that's driving you.

◆ GET INTO IT
(Making the situation your own)

1. Do you believe that you're old enough to handle all the responsibilities of adulthood? Which of these do you feel you could handle?

    a. Paying bills. ❏
    b. Marriage (which includes the joys of sexual expression). ❏
    c. Working a full-time job. ❏
    d. Keeping a budget. ❏
    e. Helping maintain a house and a car. ❏

2. In Joshua 24:15, we read that Joshua commanded the people of Israel to choose to serve either the God of the Bible or foreign gods. He said, "Choose for yourselves this day whom you will serve. . . . But as for me and my household, we will serve the LORD." The reason this is a tough choice is (check as many as you want):

a. the God of the Bible doesn't allow room for other gods. ❏
b. it's really not a tough choice at all. ❏
c. to make a choice means to be responsible for it. ❏
d. everyone will be watching to make sure that this choice is carried out. ❏
e. we'd like to be cool with God *and* keep our other gods for fun, too. ❏

◆ A WORD FROM GOD
(Getting the right message)

Trust in the LORD with all your heart and lean not on your own understanding; in all your ways acknowledge him, and he will make your paths straight. (Proverbs 3:5-6)

◆ FOR THE ROAD
(Taking something along with you)

Right now in your life you are standing at a crossroads. There are many big choices facing you. List the various areas in your life where you stand at a crossroads, and then try to decide what choices you want to make.

CONVERSATIONS WITH A TELEVISION SET
Learning to Listen

◆ICEBREAKER
(Getting your brain in gear)

Write down your most embarrassing moment at school. Some of you may want to read yours out loud.

◆TUNE IN
(Checking out the situation)

Hey! It's been a hard day. I got my shirt stuck in my locker. I stood there for five minutes trying to get the thing unjammed . . . and no matter how many times I dialed the right locker combo, it still didn't unstick the thing. I banged on it. I yelled at it. And then she walked by . . . that girl. I was so embarrassed. She was able to get the locker unstuck. I wanted to throw up.

I was five minutes late for class, which means another tardy slip, which in my case means an after-school detention. I got home at 5:00, but both my parents were still not home from work. My brother was at football practice, and I was all alone in that big lonely house. I didn't know where else to turn, so I turned on the 5:00 news.

You know, he seems like such a friendly guy, this TV anchor for a national newscast. He just looks like he'd be fun to talk to . . . so I . . . and I made sure that no one else was looking . . . turned down the sound and I started to tell him about my day. Yeah, it sounds crazy, but our conversation went kind of like this:

ME: It was a lousy day today.

HIM: Today, four hundred gorillas blew up an embassy building in Pago Pago.

ME: I got my shirt caught in my locker.

HIM: Here with this live report is our veteran overseas correspondent, Vic Traino. (Picture shifts to Pago Pago map.)

ME: Hey, where'd you go? I can't see you on the screen.

HIM (after the picture comes back to him from the map): We'll be right back after these words from our sponsors.

ME: So, this girl helped me get my shirt out of my locker. I was really embarrassed. Hey! You're gone again. What's going on? (Screen has a cereal commercial . . . then back to the newscaster.)

HIM: In other stories, authorities are saying

24

that total cleanup from last Sunday's earthquake is at least six months away.

ME: I'd still like to ask this girl out . . . but I really feel like I ought to wait until she forgets about this incident.

HIM: And now from all of us here at our newsroom, thanks for tuning us in. We really care for you. Bye!

ME: Huh? Well, thanks for listening. It's been swell.

◆JUMP IN
(Putting yourself in someone else's shoes)

1. As silly as this illustration may seem, what do you feel might be true about it? Do you ever feel lonely at home?

2. Do you believe this guy is weird because he got his shirt caught in his locker? Why or why not?

3. Have you ever felt like this guy feels right now? Describe the situation.

4. Have you ever talked to someone and felt like you were talking to a wall? How did you feel?

◆TIME OUT
(Looking at it from another point of view)

Talking to a wall. Don't deny it—you've been there. You're sharing something . . . maybe a fishing story, maybe some incredible deed you did . . . and the listener suddenly gets that glassy look in his eyes. He starts mumbling off "Uh-huhs," and you know he's gone. You feel betrayed. You feel hurt. Maybe you're talking on the phone one night and you hear nothing at the other end for a long time. You wonder if the other person has lapsed into a coma or something. AGGRAVATION! Nothing like talking to a wall.

The reason for the aggravation is simple. God wired us to want to be heard. Listening is often the language of love, and love spells effort and work. One of the best classes I ever took was with a

professional counselor who simply taught me how
to give feedback to a talker to show that person
that I was listening. It took work at first. Just tuning in always takes effort. But if listening is indeed
the language of love, then listening should be a
pursuit of every Christian, EVEN AT THE JUNIOR
HIGH AGE.

The problem, though, is that the listening
process takes a different kind of energy than what
junior high teens are cranking out these days. To
listen means, normally, that I have to stop talking.
Call me crazy! But I find that I really can't talk and
listen well at the same time. To listen means I have to
stop running. I have to look at the person . . . make
eye contact. To listen means I have to hear his story,
and not just come back with one of my own. I have
to enter his world through the door he is opening.
That's a difficult task for any junior higher.

The solution? Jesus worked very hard to
show love for people, and summed up His total
lifestyle in the verse that says, "Greater love has
no one than this, that he lay down his life for his
friends" (John 15:13). If you want to show real
love to people, some work and effort will have to
be made. And as squirmy as it might seem, that
means you're going to have to listen to people
in their time and in their way. Even the people
in your family. What an incredible challenge!
But probably better than talking to walls all
the time!!

◆GET INTO IT
(Making the situation your own)

1. In your opinion, one reason why people don't
   listen better is:

a. no time. Too busy. ❏
b. noise pollution. Who can hear anything? ❏
c. too selfish. We all have our own "fish stories" to tell. ❏
d. other _____ .

2. Name a person who you think is a super listener. Why do you feel that way about him or her?

3. What could you do that would make you be a better listener in your family setting?

a. Look at the eyes of the person who's speaking. ❏
b. Stop the person once in a while to summarize what you have heard. ❏
c. Ask questions when something seems unclear, or when further explanation is needed. ❏
d. Pray for God's help. ❏
e. Tape record what this person says so you can go over it later. ❏

4. Paul tells us to "carry each other's burdens" (Galatians 6:2). How does listening to someone help to carry that person's burden?

◆ A WORD FROM GOD
(Getting the right message)

He who answers before listening — that is his folly and his shame. (Proverbs 18:13)

◆ FOR THE ROAD
(Taking something along with you)

Sit down with a member of your class, and try practicing some of the methods listed in the last question. If you want to try something really fun, videotape the process. This gives the talker an idea what he looks like when he's talking, and what he looks like when he's listening.

ADVENTURES IN FOOD COLOR
Getting Along with Brothers and Sisters

◆ICEBREAKER
(Getting your brain in gear)

Briefly describe your brothers and sisters.

◆TUNE IN
(Checking out the situation)

Homer was a former missionary . . . but the most colorful person I have ever met. He spent his final years in our church in Dallas fully active right up to his dying day. He had a most unique gift of hospitality.

31

Once he invited my wife and me to his apartment with another couple for a Halloween party. I didn't know what to expect, but driving over we could only guess what kind of a dull affair it might be. He was an older man, and we didn't really know him that well at the time.

But when we arrived at the apartment, we were very surprised to find the door open. Inside the doorway it was pitch dark, with eerie organ music playing. Sheets were positioned so that you could only see beyond the kitchen, and they were all blowing in a mock wind that Homer conjured up with a couple of room fans.

A voice from inside said, "Take off your shoes and socks." So we did . . . and then had to wade through a very large tray of water with rice on the bottom. Yeah, it felt weird. At about this time, I was having some doubts about the man's sanity. But after we got in, he quickly turned on a light, and we all laughed . . . and yet, the really weird stuff was only beginning.

Because it was Halloween, Homer had his entire apartment decked out in orange and black. So, guess what color all the food was? The butter was orange . . . the toast was black . . . the mashed potatoes were orange . . . the hotdogs were wrapped in black licorice . . . . This guy was incredible! If he was still alive today, I'd have him working with junior high kids. People of all ages went crazy when they went to Homer's apartment for dinner. When we went over on St. Patrick's Day, all the food was green. On the Fourth of July, all the food was red, white, and blue. You never got to eat stuff in its original color.

He did everything with food color. Harmless . . . odorless . . . but it sure cast a different picture on everything. I like to enjoy the look of the food I eat. I had some squid the other night, and even though it tasted delicious, it looked awful. And Homer's food looked even worse. It is simply amazing what just a little food color can do to your system!

◆JUMP IN
(Putting yourself in someone else's shoes)

1. Name something that tastes good but looks awful.

2. Pretend that you were going to prepare a Valentine's Day meal for someone, and you wanted to play with the food color to make everything . . . well . . . pink, white, and red. How would you do it?

3. Would you like to have someone like Homer for a friend? Why or why not?

◆TIME OUT
(Looking at it from another point of view)

Just as food color changes the perspective of food, brothers and sisters change the perspective of our lives . . . for better and for worse, right? If you're honest, you'll admit to a couple of good memories with them, right? And there are probably some bad ones, too. But the point is that they change us, and as a result, we're never the same.

Fortunately, almost all the memories of time spent with my brother are positive ones. We had zillions of good times, mostly spent around sports and music . . . . And yet, the memories are mostly all good for me because I'm the older brother. I found through years of conversations with him that it's not always pleasant being on the other end. Let me explain what I mean.

Several years ago, a family asked me to counsel a nine-year-old kid who was supposed to be brilliant, but didn't pull the grades everyone knew he could. He had no interest in music or sports, and just used to sit around and veg out with video games . . . and he wasn't even very good at them.

This kid came into my office all smiles . . . but all apathy. He didn't want to do "nuthin"! The whole picture started to gel in my mind when he talked about how his older brother always got praise from the family for grades, music, sports . . . .

After the kid left my office, I called my brother long distance at his office. I told him about my appointment that morning, and I asked him to share what it was like to live in my "shadow." You see, I had a high profile growing up in both sports and music. Sometimes it seemed like my brother was shy and withdrawn. That day on the phone, though, I got a side of my brother that I had never seen before . . . and the impact of that conversation still lasts today.

Jesus had brothers and sisters. We often read about the impact of family. You can imagine how much impact He had on His family! Jesus also spoke about His *spiritual* family. He said, "Whoever does the will of my Father in heaven is my brother and sister and mother" (Matthew 12:50). His spiritual family had a great impact on His life. They shared a lot of love and laughs and sorrows as they walked the earth together.

As much as you might like to "disown" your brothers or sisters sometimes, you really can't. They will always have a part of your heart. They will always be part of your memories. They are food coloring in your life.

◆GET INTO IT
(Making the situation your own)

1. Describe a "good" moment you have had with a brother or sister.

2. Okay, now describe a "bad" moment. What made the good moment "good," and the bad moment "bad"?

3. What are the advantages of being an older brother or sister?

4. What are the advantages of being a younger brother or sister?

5. In what ways have you not been the best brother or sister that you could be?

6. We are told to "keep on loving each other as brothers" (Hebrews 13:1). In what way are all believers brothers and sisters?

◆ A WORD FROM GOD
(Getting the right message)

Be devoted to one another in brotherly love.
(Romans 12:10)

◆FOR THE ROAD
(Taking something along with you)

Find a partner this week and pretend that you are brother or sister to him or her. What problems do you think you would face if you lived in the same family? Think about what it means to be a *spiritual* brother or sister.

WHEN YOUR GENES DON'T SEEM TO FIT
Accepting Your Family Heritage

◆ICEBREAKER
(Getting your brain in gear)

On a 3 x 5 card, list some things about yourself that have to do with family background or heritage. Then shuffle the cards together and try to guess who each card is describing.

◆TUNE IN
(Checking out the situation)

A couple of years ago, I traveled with twenty high school kids to the nation of Rwanda, Africa. The day we arrived, our team went through one of the greatest culture shocks they may ever face. Being the foreigner . . . well, it was really scary.

Rwanda is a poor country, and it is an unusual sight to see a team of Americans like us all in one place over there. We drew a crowd. The special attraction, though, that got most of the comments and the attention of the crowd, was our three red-headed girls. They drew far more than their share of stares and giggles from the crowds that gathered around us. Word circulated quickly about our team, and these three girls helped create quite a stir wherever we went.

I have discovered that some red-headed girls are not all that excited to have red hair. Although most get used to it, I can remember at least one conversation with a gal who wanted to trade in her red hair. Her family told her that she needed to be proud of her red hair . . . that it marked a family resemblance dating back for generations. That bit of history gave her no comfort, though.

Maybe you have a "trait" that has been handed down to you through the years . . . or a physical mark. Maybe all your relatives are tall and you see yourself stretching upward, too. Maybe you have thick hair that curls . . . or thin hair that doesn't do anything! You might have big feet . . . a short temper . . . or a large nose. You may have gotten used to whatever trait or physical attribute you have been handed down . . . but deep down inside there might be something you want to change.

At the same time, there is an up side and a down side to all this stuff we get handed down to us. My father said that I got my teenage acne from him . . . for which I would still like to hit him after all these years. And yet, he was a superb athlete in his prime, and I have good memories of the sports that I have been involved in through the years. I have broken par on a real golf course . . . and enjoyed success as a baseball pitcher. Both good and bad stuff come from your parents. Yeah, I guess it was worth enduring the zits!

40

◆ JUMP IN
(Putting yourself in someone else's shoes)

1. Okay, name those distinctive things you inherited from your parents. Just to give you some starters, how about:

   a. eye color?

   b. hair color?

   c. unique features?

   d. temperament?

   e. talents?

2. If you could change any of these things about you, what would you change?

3. If you could trade any attribute or physical characteristic with someone in the room, what would you trade away and trade for?

◆TIME OUT
(Looking at it from another point of view)

Just in case you think that you are the only teen in America who thinks that he would like to change his looks . . . or something about himself . . . think again. To some degree, we all have areas we would like to change. I have made several recordings, but I don't like my voice. I have heard the testimony of one beauty queen who told a reporter that she thought she was ugly. Some of your most talented people may feel like they are absolutely ungifted and struggling in their fields.

One reason for this is that we live in a world of comparisons . . . and we spend our time not living up to the model our heroes portray. Chances are that you will never live up to the glitz and glamour that media stars seem to have, and if you follow in the footsteps of so many in our world, you'll find yourself on the short end of the identity stick . . . always looking in your mirror and cursing God because of your big nose.

We have all heard the statement, "God doesn't make junk, and didn't start when He made you."

That really doesn't help, does it? If we feel inadequate . . . ugly . . . too short . . . too fat . . . then some cutesy statement like "God doesn't make junk" only makes us feel guiltier. Now all of a sudden we have the problem of not only being dissatisfied with our looks . . . but we also have the problem of arguing with God. "Well, yes, God, You did make junk. Just look at me." Some kids even get mad at their parents for their looks or their temper . . . or whatever. You would think that there has to be an answer to this dilemma, and there is. But it isn't easy.

First . . . and this is going to blow you away . . . I have yet to meet an absolutely ugly person. Because we make what I call relative comparisons, we usually think: "I am not good looking because I am not as good looking as _____ ." Comparisons like this are a no-win situation. There will always be someone we don't think we can measure up to. And so we develop a spirit that is never content. The Bible tells us that the right kind of contentment will really add a lot to our lives (1 Timothy 6:6). God can give us contentment, but it doesn't come easy in a world that makes comparisons all the time.

Second, think about the time and effort that goes into most of the photos in the media. A good friend of mine is a photographer. He told me once that out of about 150 pictures he takes, he might keep one. One! Hey, how about if we get to see all the boo boos . . . you know . . . eyes closed and all that stuff. Models work for hours to get a certain look, and just the right lighting. Yes, it's a lot different than the shots Dad takes through his Instamatic on vacations, isn't it?

Third, in a world of relative comparisons, God's

Word is not relative. This is hard to take, because we don't have absolutes in this world to compare to. Everything in our world is measured against something that changes. The one measuring standard that doesn't change is the Bible. Because we aren't used to something that doesn't change, we have a hard time handling statements from a book of absolutes.

In other words, God doesn't lie. God isn't wrong. His Word says all kinds of things about you. It says that you are "fearfully and wonderfully made" (Psalm 139:14).

David was the one who made that statement. I would guess that David had moments when he got really ticked off about certain things about himself. His life was full of struggles. There was an up side: he had the courage to face a giant. There was a down side: he committed adultery. The inconsistency must have driven him nuts, because he was "a man after God's own heart" (Acts 13:22).

God understands our struggles to come to self-acceptance. He doesn't want us to lose heart during our teen years. If we spend our time in comparisons that are always changing, we'll never be content. But if we spend more time in that unchanging measuring instrument, the Word of God, we'll find both contentment and acceptance.

◆GET INTO IT
(Making the situation your own)

1. In Psalm 139:13-14, David says to God, "You created my inmost being; you knit me together in my mother's womb. I praise you because I am

fearfully and wonderfully made." Can you give thanks to God for who you are? Why or why not?

2. Someone you know is dissatisfied because he has a large nose. He should:

   a. simply mope through life in a hopeless situation. ❏
   b. get a nose job. ❏
   c. not get so wrapped up in his looks. ❏
   d. spend more time reading his Bible. ❏

3. Are you "content" with your physical appearance? What things can you change and what things cannot be changed?

4. What things could you do to work toward a spirit of contentment?

   a. Watch less TV. ❏
   b. Be less image-conscious and focus on inner changes. ❏
   c. Spend more time reading your Bible. ❏
   d. Other _____ .

5. How does the way you are on the inside affect your appearance on the outside?

◆ A WORD FROM GOD
(Getting the right message)

The LORD does not look at the things man looks at. Man looks at the outward appearance, but the LORD looks at the heart. (1 Samuel 16:7)

◆ FOR THE ROAD
(Taking something along with you)

There's a saying, "You are what you eat." Describe yourself and your view of yourself in terms of your favorite magazines, books, movies, music, and tastes in fashion. After describing yourself this way, state why you are not content with yourself, even the trends you are practicing. What would it take to make you content?

WOULD SOMEONE PLEASE TURN THIS FAMILY OFF!
Finding Calm in the Middle of the Storm

◆ICEBREAKER
(Getting your brain in gear)

Get everybody in the group talking at the same time (that shouldn't be too hard). While all this confusion is going on all around you, try your best to feel at peace or at rest. Pretty hard, isn't it?

◆TUNE IN
(Checking out the situation)

No fooling. I love my microwave. On behalf of the men of America who burn Jell-O when they cook, I want to express my gratitude for the microwave. My wife and daughter recently went to San Diego to visit family, leaving me to play bachelor for a few days. Bachelor means that I run around twice as fast as I normally do, and food is something I catch on the run.

Due to the amazing leftovers my wife leaves me in times like this, usually neatly labeled with

47

instructions, I am able to eat like an elephant. No, this doesn't mean I eat grass, peanuts, or leaves from trees. The way I was headed, though, I'd be equal in size to an elephant in about ten years time.

The genius of these leftovers is in the microwave. I could slap in everything from beef brisket to macaroni and cheese, and in just a couple of minutes I was looking at an instant meal. Why, if TV got really dull, I would throw something in just to watch it blow up. Take it out, clean off the sides and the door, and do it again.

The microwave is an indicator of the pulse of the American family today. Fast! We've invented other things that have also made life faster, therefore making us more efficient . . . that is, in our own minds—computers, fast-food restaurants, the fast-forward button on the remote control . . . .

One of my favorites is the car phone. We youth pastors are totally the executive type, so we understand the need for car phones today. I am heading home from the office and get stuck in bumper-to-bumper traffic. I decide to make the best use of my time, so I pull out my car phone, and for just mega bucks per call, I dial a few people up to ask them how they're doing.

During one call, I really get involved in the conversation . . . a seventh grader confessing that he owns drug plantations in Colombia. I get so engrossed with his story that I neglect to see the brake lights in front of me, and I plow my 1981 Dodge into the back of a Lamborghini. But it's no sweat. I give the owner of the Lamborghini the deed to my house, my first-born child, and the promise that I will mow his grass using only my mouth for the rest of my life. Uh, wait a minute. Was that supposed to be more efficient?

◆ JUMP IN
(Putting yourself in someone else's shoes)

1. Describe what life in your house would be like with:

   a. no microwave.

   b. no bathroom with a flush toilet.

   c. no television.

2. If life today is supposed to be more efficient, more convenient, and so on, then why do you think it's more busy?

3. Doesn't it make sense that if life is more efficient than it used to be, we should have more time for rest? Why, then, is everyone so tired?

49

4. If you could name one new gadget that you could invent to make life easier in the next ten years (and please be as silly as you'd like on this question), what would you invent?

◆TIME OUT
(Looking at it from another point of view)

Families are tired. *Teens* are tired! They go on retreats (supposedly times of rest) with youth groups or school groups, and come back wiped out . . . although, come to think of it, it is cool to show up on Monday morning tired from the weekend.

You can see it, can't you? Three friends sharing the stories of their weekends. One says, "Man, I'm so tired. My dad made me rake leaves for half an hour on Saturday morning. I need a couple of weeks off." Another says, "That's nothing. I went to a party on Saturday night and didn't get home until Sunday afternoon. I need a year off!" A third one says, "That's nothing. I had to go to a *family reunion*! I'm checking into the intensive care unit this afternoon. I might not ever be back."

Even though everyone has plenty to do these days, no one seems to be willing to pull the plug and stop this merry-go-round of busy-ness. So you go to school with your tired stories, find other tired people who are equally busy and equally wiped out, and you just keep on going. Your parents do it. Your brothers and sisters do it. Your hamster does it. You do it.

◆ GET INTO IT
(Making the situation your own)

1. Why do you think so many teens are always "tired"?

2. If there was one thing you could cut out of your schedule right now, what would it be?

3. Do you feel your parents are too busy? Why or why not?

4. The Bible has a lot to say about working and resting. What do you think about this verse?

"By the seventh day God had finished the work he had been doing; so on the seventh day he rested from all his work" (Genesis 2:2).

◆ A WORD FROM GOD
(Getting the right message)

"Come to me, all you who are weary and burdened, and I will give you rest." (Matthew 11:28)

◆ FOR THE ROAD
(Taking something along with you)

Sit down with your parents and list everything you do. Then, with their help, *prioritize* your activities. In other words, list them in order of importance. Now, simplify your life by cutting out one or two of your activities.